POLICE PUBLIC CALL BOX

POLICE TELEPHONE
FREE
FOR USE OF
PUBLIC
ADVICE & ASSISTANCE
OBTAINABLE IMMEDIATELY

OFFICERS & CARS
RESPOND TO ALL CALLS
PULL TO OPEN

MEET THE ELEVENTH DOCTOR

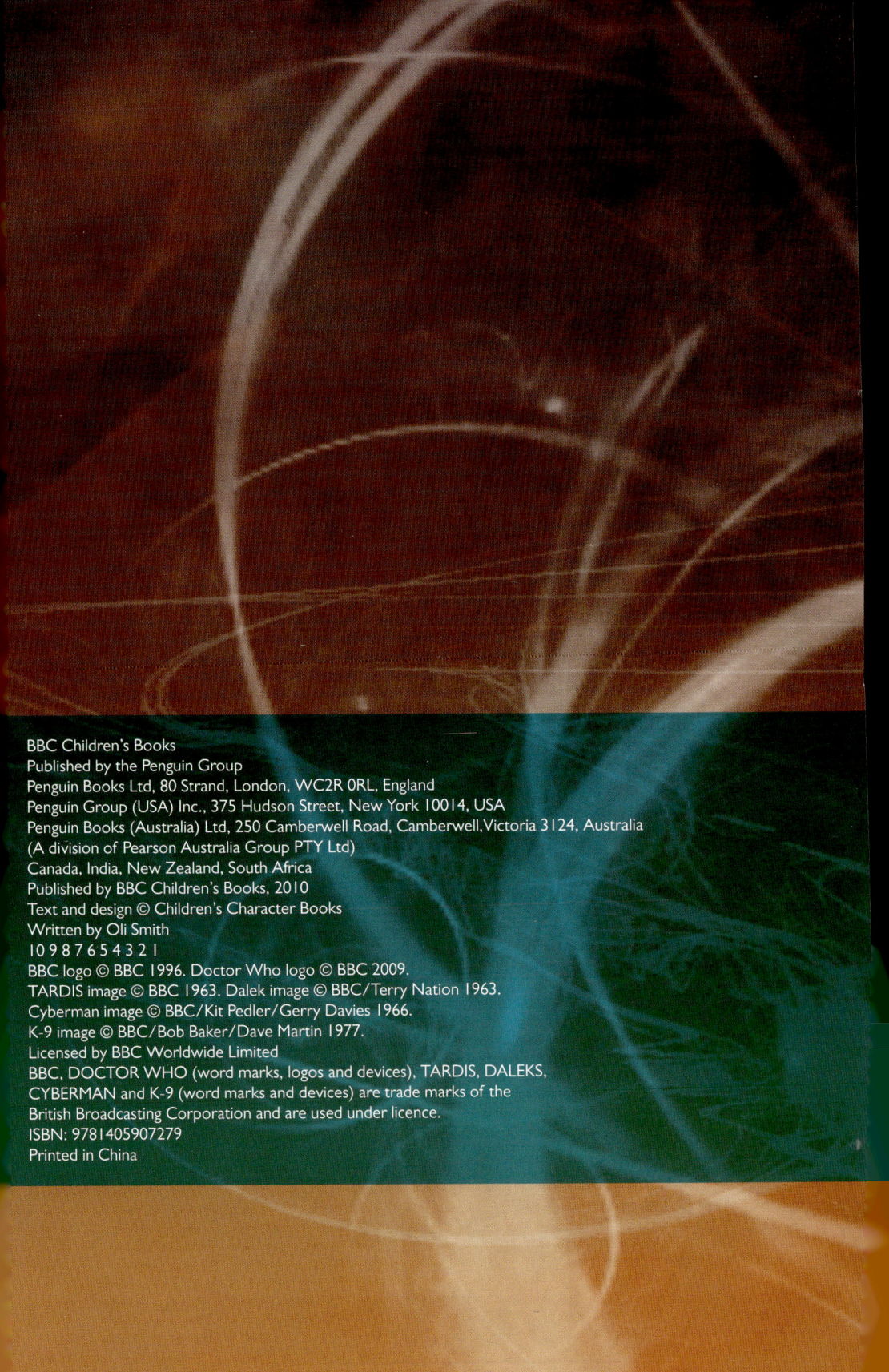

BBC Children's Books
Published by the Penguin Group
Penguin Books Ltd, 80 Strand, London, WC2R 0RL, England
Penguin Group (USA) Inc., 375 Hudson Street, New York 10014, USA
Penguin Books (Australia) Ltd, 250 Camberwell Road, Camberwell, Victoria 3124, Australia
(A division of Pearson Australia Group PTY Ltd)
Canada, India, New Zealand, South Africa
Published by BBC Children's Books, 2010
Text and design © Children's Character Books
Written by Oli Smith
10 9 8 7 6 5 4 3 2 1

ISBN: 9781405907279
Printed in China

CONTENTS

MEET THE
ELEVENTH DOCTOR!

Who is the Doctor?

Even now, as we follow the Doctor through his eleventh incarnation, little is known about this mysterious wanderer. We know that he is the last of his kind, that he abhors violence, that he loves to travel and explore and that his manner and dress is often eccentric. But there is also a darker side to the Doctor's life: It has been said that death is his constant companion and that he keeps moving on because he daren't look back. There are many myths and legends that surround the Doctor but, at the heart of the story and in the Time Lord's own words, he is simply, "a madman with a box."

Why does he travel?

In his TARDIS, a time and space ship that is bigger inside than out, the Doctor is able to go to any planet in the universe and to any point in that planet's existence – but somehow he always seems to find trouble wherever he lands. On occasion it has been hinted that the Doctor is deliberately seeking out wrongs to be righted, on others it seems that the TARDIS itself is the one transporting the Time Lord to times and places where he can do some good, but most of the time it seems that his erratic steering of the TARDIS simply drops him into such situations by chance. The Doctor himself seems to prefer the latter and revels in the opportunity to visit places and times he might otherwise have never known existed.

Regeneration!

As a Time Lord the Doctor not only has an incredibly long lifespan, but also the ability to cheat death. When his body is killed he is able to restructure his cells and become, literally, a new man. With his dangerous lifestyle, the Doctor has needed to call upon this power ten times and only at the end of his first incarnation has he ever simply 'worn' a body out. But despite often being cut down in his prime, (and indeed some incarnations of the Doctor appear to have lasted only a handful of years), he has still managed to reach nine hundred and seven years old.

Like the regeneration from his seventh incarnation to his eighth, the Tenth Doctor's transition to the Eleventh took several hours to occur. Unwilling to go without a fight, his tenth incarnation held on long enough to say goodbye to his companions, before releasing the pent-up regeneration energy in a cascade that almost destroyed the TARDIS. This left the confused Eleventh Doctor only a few seconds to check his new body before attempting to regain control of the damaged ship, as it plunged towards Earth.

His Character

Despite his disappointment at *still* not being ginger, the Eleventh Doctor seemed more confident in his new body than his previous two incarnations. The events of the Tenth Doctor's final days appeared to have given him a sense of closure on the Time War and the loss of his people, and he embarked on his new life without the guilt and vulnerability that had burdened his ninth and tenth incarnations. Like a gentleman explorer of old, the Eleventh Doctor bounds through his adventures with enthusiasm, wonder and an air of authority, but he's also unwilling to be taken advantage of and quick to condemn people who stand in his way with a sharp put-down.

Despite making full use of his youthful body, he has the air of an old man about him, which is reflected in his vintage dress sense, and his mature persona is tempered with a child-like wonder.

The Time Lords

Hailing from the planet of Gallifrey in the constellation of Kasterborous, the Time Lords were imbued with the power to see time in a way that no other race could; they can see the past, the present and the future; what could be and what must. It is an ability that the Doctor has often described as a curse. But despite their power, the Time Lords remained apart from the rest of the universe, content simply to observe. Eventually, their idle lifestyle drove the First Doctor to steal his TARDIS and leave his home planet in search of adventure and excitement and during his absence, the once noble race's isolation transformed them into a corrupt and petty society. Despite returning in his fourth incarnation to be elected President of the High Council of Time Lords, the Doctor was too ashamed of his own people to assert his authority and fled once more.

The Time War

The Time Lords were unable to remain uninvolved forever, and soon they were forced into a war with the vast forces of the Dalek Empire, a race that embodied evil. The Doctor was called to the front line, and even his arch enemy, the Master, was resurrected and given a new set of regenerations as they fought together across the stars and out of time. But things took a turn for the worse when the resurrected Rassilon, founder of Time Lord Civilisation, became President of the High Council. Having decided that there was no way to win the war he decreed that it would be better to destroy time itself than let the war continue. At the last minute, the Doctor used a device known only as 'The Moment', to place the war in a Time Lock, apart from the rest of the universe. In a last ditch attempt to carry out his plan, Rassilon used the Master to break the lock, but as Gallifrey returned in the skies above Earth, the Master turned on the President, severing his link to the universe, and sending Gallifrey hurtling back into the Time War.

His Enemies

The Doctor once said that, "you can always judge a man by the quality of his enemies," and if that is so the Doctor ranks up there with the best of them. Over the years he has fought gods and demons, entire armies of ruthless Daleks and emotionless Cybermen, and saved Earth more times than anybody can remember.

It is the Master, though, who has always remained the Doctor's deadliest foe, causing the deaths of both his fourth and seventh incarnations as well as aiding in the series of events that lead to the death of the Tenth Doctor.

During their time on Gallifrey, the Doctor and the Master had once been the greatest of friends, until the Master was driven mad as a child when he looked into the Untempered Schism and saw time itself. The ultimate survivor, the Master was resurrected to fight in the Time War, little knowing that his race had other plans for him.

His Allies

The Doctor has never liked to travel alone, and believes that his adventuring is always more enjoyable when experienced with someone else. Initially travelling with his granddaughter Susan, the Doctor has had many companions over the centuries – both human and alien, including K-9 – his faithful robot dog, and Brigadier Lethbridge-Stewart – one of the only people to have ever been lucky enough to encounter the Doctor in almost all of his regenerations.

But as he got older, the Doctor began to get tired of watching his companions grow old whilst he remained ageless, and after experiencing the devastating losses of both Rose and Donna he eventually decided that it was safer to travel alone. But it soon became clear that the temptation to take things too far grew too great if there was no one there to stop him.

THE TARDIS

POLICE PUBLIC CALL BOX

POLICE PUBLIC CALL BOX

POLICE TELEPHONE
FREE
FOR USE OF
PUBLIC
ADVICE & ASSISTANCE
OBTAINABLE IMMEDIATELY
OFFICERS & CARS
RESPOND TO ALL CALLS
PULL TO OPEN

The TARDIS (which stands for Time And Relative Dimension In Space) is the Time Lord's oldest and most faithful companion. While Doctors might come and go, his ship remains firmly stuck in the shape of an old-fashioned 1950s Police Box. But that doesn't mean that its vast interior hasn't had a few makeovers over the years…

The First Doctor's TARDIS was rather out of date when he stole it, compared to the other time machines available at the time. An old Type 40, the TARDIS appears to be rather eccentric and is often never quite able to arrive in the right place or the right time. Occasionally the Doctor has tried to repair his ship, to varying degrees of success, but most of the time it seems that he quite enjoys the random nature of his travels and the opportunity to discover new races and planets that he might otherwise have missed.

It was revealed during the Tenth Doctor's incarnation that TARDISes were actually grown on Gallifrey rather than built, which means that it is unlikely we will ever see another in a universe without the Time Lords.

The Doctor's TARDIS seems to have been modified somewhat since the Time War, and is no longer powered by the Eye of Harmony, a black hole that had been trapped in the heart of Gallifrey and which powered the whole of Time Lord society. Instead, the ship refuels by landing on rifts in time and space and soaking up the residual time energy like a sponge.

Redecorating

Every TARDIS is equipped with a chameleon circuit that allows its exterior form to change and blend into its surroundings wherever and whenever it lands. Unfortunately, the chameleon circuit on the Doctor's TARDIS is one of the many things about it that has broken down and it has remained stuck as a Police Box ever since the Doctor landed in London in 1963. But although the exterior circuits have been broken, the Doctor has been known to redesign the interior of his ship many times over the years.

From its initial appearance as a large white laboratory, replete with banks of extra equipment and space age furnishings, the TARDIS control room has evolved into a sleek and elegant space – from a console covered in keypads to a gothic Victorian palace – it has always retained the familiar hexagonal console, roundels and, surprisingly, an old hat stand. There have been many glimpses of other rooms in the TARDIS; bedrooms, wardrobes, secondary control rooms, even a swimming pool and a library (both of which unexpectedly merged after the Eleventh Doctor's regeneration) have been spotted in its labyrinthine corridors.

A TARDIS was originally designed to be flown by six crewmembers, one for each side of the console, so the Doctor has occasionally had to improvise extra controls from whatever he has had lying around to enable him to fly it solo. Despite that, it's rarely a smooth ride with the Doctor at the helm.

THE TARDIS REGENERATED

The death of the Tenth Doctor took its toll on the TARDIS and, in the violence of the regeneration, as the Time Lord's body exploded with the energy he had held back just long enough to bid farewell to his friends, the control room disintegrated around him. But, like the Doctor himself, the TARDIS too was capable of regeneration and its battle-worn interior was replaced with a majestic space, which incorporated elements of everything that had come before. Even its battered Police Box shell was replaced with a fresher, cleaner, younger model, in a style that reflected the personality of its new pilot.

The pool beneath the console is a condensate of the fuel that powers the TARDIS, and is fed through pipes into the central column.

The central column, sometimes known as the time rotor, is the heart of the TARDIS' engines, rising and falling whilst the ship is in flight.

The monitor is the Doctor's main source of information, capable of exhibiting communications and statistics whilst the Time Lord works at the console.

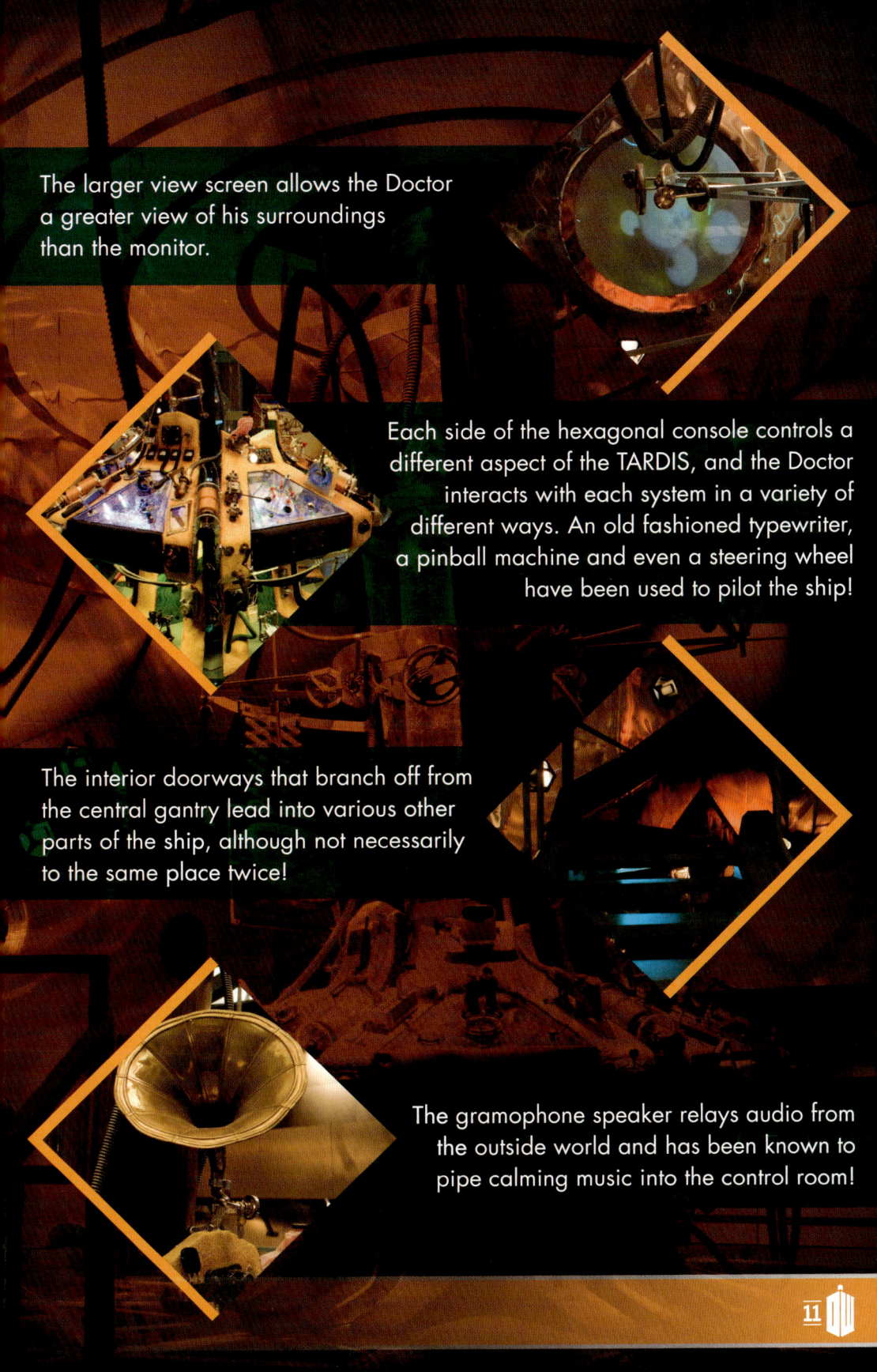

The larger view screen allows the Doctor a greater view of his surroundings than the monitor.

Each side of the hexagonal console controls a different aspect of the TARDIS, and the Doctor interacts with each system in a variety of different ways. An old fashioned typewriter, a pinball machine and even a steering wheel have been used to pilot the ship!

The interior doorways that branch off from the central gantry lead into various other parts of the ship, although not necessarily to the same place twice!

The gramophone speaker relays audio from the outside world and has been known to pipe calming music into the control room!

TARDIS TECHNOLOGY

Apart from the main control room, the TARDIS is home to some fascinating technology. Some are based on Gallifreyan science, but others have been designed specifically by the Doctor to aid him in his adventures and have, over time, become a part of the ship itself.

THE CLOISTER BELL

First heard during the Fourth Doctor's final adventure, the cloister bell sounds when the TARDIS is in mortal danger. Its funereal tone has also been known to herald the end of the universe or the imminent death of the Doctor.

THE CHAMELEON CIRCUIT

Originally designed to morph the exterior of the TARDIS into an object that blends in with its surroundings, the Doctor's TARDIS has become so used to its own damaged chameleon circuit that the interior doors have changed to match the exterior. The interface between the TARDIS control room and the outside universe is protected by an oxygen shield which can be expanded beyond the doors.

THE CHAMELEON ARCH

Working in much the same way as the TARDIS' Chameleon Circuit, the Chameleon Arch changes the biological make up of a Time Lord into that of another species, creating a history, personality and a false set of memories to match. The original Time Lord's essence is preserved inside a special artefact disguised as a fob watch which, when opened, will fully restore the user to his or her original state.

THE SONIC SCREWDRIVER

Built by the Doctor during his second incarnation, the sonic screwdriver is the Doctor's all-purpose tool; helping him to escape prisons, disable androids and block teleports amongst its many other functions and settings. It was destroyed during the Fifth Doctor's era then rebuilt by the Seventh, but by the time of the Ninth Doctor's incarnation it had become such a useful ally that the TARDIS developed the capacity to grow him a new one in the event of its destruction. With the newly-regenerated TARDIS came a new improved sonic screwdriver. This version sports an emerald tip behind its unfolding latch mechanism and plugs into the TARDIS console.

THE PSYCHIC PAPER

Its exact origins are unknown, but the psychic paper is one of the Doctor's most valuable tools. Capable of forging any document that fits onto its white slip, the Doctor uses it often to create fake identities that help him to get straight into the middle of the action. Over time the psychic paper has developed a special link with the Time Lord, allowing him to receive messages from across the stars.

THE VISUAL RECOGNITION SYSTEM

A present from the Doctor's godmother, this device is capable of scanning any alien that looks into its mirrored screen and identifying its race, planet of origin and any other distinguishing characteristics. Used by the Doctor to identify the Krafayis that was threatening van Gogh, its screen was also capable of reflecting a visible image of the invisible creature.

TARDIS TRAVELLERS

The Doctor is always at his best whilst travelling with companions and his eleventh incarnation is no exception.

Amy Pond

It seemed clear from the moment that the Doctor met the young Amelia that she was destined to travel with him and her wish was finally granted when he appeared with a new TARDIS and his regeneration finally complete. It is unclear if the Doctor knew the link between Amy and the crack in the universe, but it certainly came as a surprise when he realised that she was due to be married the day after she ran away.

Out of all the Doctor's companions, it is Amy's life upon which he has had the most impact. She has experienced a future of domestic bliss whilst under the influence of the Dream Lord, watched her fiancé die more than once, and even had her missing parents resurrected as the universe was reborn. Amy has taken these events in her stride, using the tragedies to grow stronger and help her decide once and for all who she cares about most; Rory, or the Doctor.

River Song

River's relationship with the Doctor is as complicated as their meetings. Never quite in the right order, the Tenth Doctor has already experienced her death, but when she tricks the Doctor into helping her fight the Weeping Angels, she is already aware of a much deeper connection between the two of them. This time it is revealed that River Song possesses a dark secret, which she seems very keen to keep the Doctor in the dark about.

When the events that lead to the end of the universe began, she set off to help the Doctor uncover the mysteries of the Pandorica. It's uncertain what happened to River when the universe was remade, but she hinted that all would be revealed soon.

Rory Williams

Amy's long-suffering fiancé, Rory was inspired to become a nurse at the local hospital after years of playing the 'Raggedy Doctor' with Amy as a child. Surprised at his stag-do by the Time Lord, Rory joined the TARDIS team to discover that the Doctor and Amy have kissed.

But time seemed to heal all wounds and soon the trio were getting on famously – becoming the ultimate TARDIS crew. After his death was foreshadowed when they met the sinister Dream Lord, Rory was shot during a battle with an underground tribe of Silurians and became another victim of the sinister crack in the universe; erased from both history and his fiancé's memory…

When the young man was finally reunited with the Doctor, it was through extraordinary means. Part of a trap concocted by the Time Lord's deadliest foes, Rory was resurrected from Amy's memories into the body of a plastic Auton! Disguised as a Roman soldier, Rory protected Amy as she was suspended in the Pandorica, following it wherever it went for nearly two thousand years.

Vincent van Gogh

Vincent may only have been a temporary traveller in the Doctor's time machine, but the revelation that his work would have such an impact on the world of art, despite the harsh criticism that he suffered in his own time, inspired him to transform the final year of his life into his most productive ever. Amy was heartbroken to find that his visit to the future was not enough to prevent Vincent's eventual suicide. His mind was too broken to be healed by the discovery that his work would make him immortal.

The Eleventh Hour

As a young girl, Amelia Pond is worrying about the crack in her wall, when the TARDIS suddenly crashes into her back garden in the middle of the night.

The newly-regenerated Eleventh Doctor hauls himself out of his broken spaceship and it is only a few minutes before he is trying to solve the mystery of the crack in the universe. He is shocked to discover a prison cell on the other side, through which a huge eye warns him that, "Prisoner Zero has escaped." Rushing back to the TARDIS to try and stabilise the regenerating machine, he accidentally travels twelve years into the future before promptly being arrested by the grown-up Amy dressed as a policewoman. Together they discover that Prisoner Zero has been holed up in a mysterious hidden room in Amy's house. But the threat of the multi-form is soon overshadowed by the arrival of an Atraxi ship, threatening to destroy the planet unless they hand the multi-form Prisoner Zero over.

Together with Amy's boyfriend, Rory, and computer geek Jeff, the Doctor manages to trick the multi-form into announcing itself to the Atraxi just in time to prevent the world from being incinerated. But as the ship is about to leave, the Doctor summons the aliens back, demanding that they promise to never return – the Eleventh Doctor has arrived and as he enters his newly-regenerated TARDIS, he decides to take her for a quick spin, which lasts two years for poor Amy Pond.

On the eve of her wedding, Amy hears a familiar noise in the garden and, with her white dress left hanging on the back of her wardrobe, she rushes to the TARDIS to join the Doctor on his adventures.

The Beast Below

The Doctor and Amy arrive on Starship UK, a massive spacecraft built to escape the solar flares that engulf Earth in the far future. Immediately, they realise that something is wrong. A police state is in force and the whole ship is watched over by the sinister Smilers.

Whilst investigating, Amy discovers an alien tentacle sprouting from the ground and is lead to a voting chamber where the ghastly secret of the Starship is explained to her. Like the rest of the ship's population, she chooses to forget what she has seen, but when the Doctor vetoes her decision the pair are dropped into the mouth of a massive beast situated in the underbelly of the ship.

They are saved by Liz Ten, the current Queen of England, and together they travel to the Tower of London in search of an explanation. The Winders, guardians of the ship's secret, reveal that the ship is not powered by traditional engines and instead has been built on top of an enormous Star Whale, the last of its kind. They have been torturing the poor creature, forcing it to transport them through space and the Doctor is outraged when he realises that he has to choose between the human race and the Star Whale.

At the last minute, Amy discovers one other alternative; that the Star Whale approached Earth out of compassion, to save them from the solar flares. She shuts down the Tower of London and the humans realise that they needn't harm the beast any longer.

Victory of the Daleks

At the request of Prime Minister Winston Churchill, the TARDIS lands in a secret war cabinet at the height of the London Blitz. The Doctor discovers that the allies' new secret weapon, the Ironsides, is in fact a trio of Daleks. Supposedly created by Professor Bracewell, the Ironsides initially appear docile and completely dedicated to helping the British win the war. But once the Doctor confronts them, demanding that they acknowledge that they are Daleks and that he is their mortal enemy, they reveal their sinister plan.

Professor Bracewell is an android, built by the Daleks to help them infiltrate the War Cabinet in the knowledge that the Doctor would eventually find them. And when the Time Lord follows them to their orbiting spacecraft, he is shocked to discover a Dalek Progenitor, primed and ready to rebuild the Dalek Empire. The Progenitor had refused to acknowledge that these scavengers were Daleks, because their DNA had become too corrupted after centuries of struggling to survive. They required the testimony of the Doctor to be accepted.

The Progenitor activates, spewing forth a grand new race of Daleks. Tall, sleek and imposing, the Doctor's enemies have never been so dangerous. Desperate to halt the birth of this new race, the Doctor calls upon Bracewell to use the Dalek technology against them, sending a squad of spitfires into space, encased in gravity bubbles. The Dalek ship is disabled but manages to flee into the Time Vortex. Earth might be safe for now, but the Doctor is sure that it is only a matter of time before the Daleks return…

The Daleks are the Doctor's oldest foes and he has fought them throughout every one of his incarnations. Created by the crippled genius Davros, they are one of the only races to successfully master time travel. Their uniformity and passionate hatred of anything different represents everything that the Doctor despises. Seemingly indestructible, they have returned time after time whilst the Doctor loses everything.

The Daleks – Reborn!

The new breed of Daleks embody the most powerful and evil aspects of their race. Standing over six feet tall, the design of their outer casing harks back to their earliest encounters with the First Doctor, and their stature and colouring is reminiscent of the Daleks that first populated Skaro after their war with the Thals. In fact, this race still retains their original biological eyeballs embedded into the eyestalk – a grotesque reminder that they were once flesh and blood.

Smooth and elegant, the different primary colours of their armour denote their rank and role in the new Dalek Empire.

WHITE – THE SUPREME

YELLOW – THE ETERNAL

RED – THE DRONE

BLUE – THE STRATEGIST

ORANGE – THE SCIENTIST

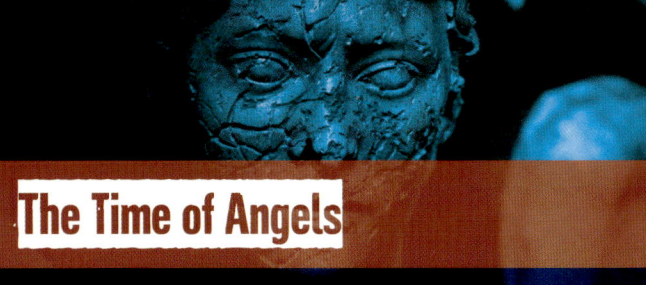

The Time of Angels

Whilst visiting a museum, the Doctor receives a message that summons him to a specific point in time and space. He is shocked to encounter River Song as she hurtles into the TARDIS to escape a daring break-in on the doomed *Byzantium* spaceship. As the ship crashes onto an alien planet, the Doctor is introduced to Father Octavian and his squad of Clerics. Together with River, they have been charged with destroying the ship's cargo, a deadly Weeping Angel.

The group are forced to navigate a maze of catacombs to attempt to reach the wreckage of the ship, and in doing so, stumble upon the remains of an army of Weeping Angels. The Angel in the hold had crashed the ship deliberately, so that its comrades could feed off the ship's energy and regain their strength. As the team approach the ship, they are taunted by the voice of a dead Cleric, Bob, his vocal chords manipulated at the hands of their hunters.

Surrounded beneath the hull of the ship by the grotesque remnants of the statues, they appear to be facing certain death.

Flesh and Stone

At the last minute, the Doctor reverses the gravity – inverting the team so that they are standing on the hull. As they descend into the *Byzantium* and flee into the oxygen forest at the heart of the ship, the angels reveal that there is more energy on board than simply the engines. The Doctor is shocked to discover the presence of a crack, identical to the one on Amy's bedroom wall.

As the Doctor and River desperately attempt to come up with a plan to defeat the Angels, Amy is left stranded and blind in the forest with a Weeping Angel trapped in the corner of her eye, counting her down to death. Suddenly the crack opens and emits a deadly wave of time energy, absorbing anything that stands in its way and erasing them from time and space. Suddenly scared, the Angels try to throw the Doctor into the chasm, in the hope that his Time Lord nature will close the gap. But before they can do so, the artificial gravity on the ship cuts out, sending the Angels tumbling into the crack and sealing it permanently.

The Angel in her eye is erased from time and Amy is set free. As she returns home on the day that she left, she reveals that she is getting married in the morning before suddenly kissing the Doctor!

The Weeping Angels were first seen in the adventure 'Blink'. The ultimate predator, they exist only whilst unobserved and this quantum lock causes them to turn to stone the instant they are seen.

The Vampires of Venice

The Doctor gatecrashes Rory's stag-do in an attempt to make amends for the accidental kiss he shared with Amy, and offers to take the pair on a date. He whisks them off to Venice in 1580, where the city has been put under quarantine for fear of the plague, despite the fact that the disease had died out years ago. Intrigued, the trio discover that aquatic vampires are running the city, lead by Rosanna, a Sister of the Water and mother of the Saturnynes. Using the Calvierri School for Girls as a front, she has been taking young women from the city and converting them into Sisters in an attempt to rebuild her lost race. Only the male of the species survived the escape from Saturnyne and are hiding in the Venetian canals, but soon she will have created enough females to breed a new civilisation.

With the help of Guido, the father of one of the sisters, Amy becomes a pupil at the school, allowing the Doctor entry into their inner sanctum. He discovers that their plan is to sink Venice by creating the greatest storm of all, but as dark clouds descend upon the city, Guido manages to destroy the converted sisters, killing himself in the explosion. Her plan foiled, Rosanna leaves the city to the mercy of the elements, throwing herself upon the ravenous jaws of her children, but at the last minute the Doctor manages to switch off her generator and disperse the clouds.

As the sun returns and Venice is freed, the Doctor and Amy invite Rory to continue travelling with them – an offer he can't refuse.

Amy's Choice

Five years into their future, a pregnant Amy and ponytail sporting Rory have settled down together in Leadworth when the Doctor comes to visit and suddenly the world turns on its head. The trio awake to find themselves once more in the TARDIS, convinced that the events in the village were nothing but a dream.

But when each member of the TARDIS crew realises that they are sharing the same experiences, the Doctor suspects that something sinister is going on. The three of them are living two parallel existences, flitting between a future Leadworth and the TARDIS seemingly at random, and both worlds contain hidden dangers.

As the TARDIS controls are overridden by a mysterious entity known only as the Dream Lord and the ship is sent spinning towards a frozen sun, the old people of Leadworth reveal themselves to be possessed by the bitter refugees of a lost race of sinister aliens. The Dream Lord presents them with a simple puzzle, one of the worlds is a dream and to escape it they have to die, but if they choose wrong then they will die for real.

Too scared to act for fear of choosing wrongly, it is only when Rory is killed by alien venom in Leadworth that Amy makes the ultimate decision. If Rory is dead in this world then she would rather die than live in it. The Doctor and Amy make the ultimate sacrifice and fortunately wake up inside a freezing TARDIS with Rory.

But the Doctor isn't convinced they've escaped, as the Dream Lord was so desperate for them to choose that he suspects that neither world is truly real. He sets the controls to blow up the TARDIS and Amy, Rory and the Doctor wake up once more in the real control room. The Doctor finds a speck of psychic pollen, excited into producing a dream-state by the time rotor, and explains how it fed off his memories and fears to produce both worlds; the Dream Lord was the Doctor's subconscious.

The Hungry Earth

The Doctor, Amy and Rory arrive in the remote Welsh town of Cwmtaff in 2020, where an elaborate mining operation is underway. Investigating strange landmarks and mineral deposits, the drilling team don't realise that they have disturbed something beneath the surface until it is too late. As the Doctor investigates the mining complex, he is unable to save Amy from being pulled into the ground, and as the town becomes enclosed by an impenetrable force field, he realises that something is drilling *up* to meet them.

Barricading themselves in the church, the Doctor, Rory and the villagers attempt to set up a surveillance system, which is immediately disabled as a strange reptilian creature breaks the surface. After a struggle in which a man, Tony, is stung, the group manage to capture the creature and the Doctor realises that she is a member of a tribe of Homo Reptilia.

Leaving the creature in the hands of Rory and the villagers, the Doctor and project leader Nasreen use the TARDIS to descend into the creatures' underground city, to try to save Amy before she is dissected as part of the Homo Reptilia's research.

Originally known as the Silurians, the Doctor encountered a tribe of Homo Reptilia during his third incarnation whilst working for UNIT, as well as another tribe known as the Sea Devils shortly afterwards. They combined forces during the Fifth Doctor's era in a joint attack on an undersea base, but on all three occasions a peace agreement between the humans and the reptilians was unattainable and the tribes were destroyed.

Cold Blood

As alarms sound to alert the Homo Reptilia to the Doctor's arrival, Amy and fellow prisoner Mo manage to escape. But they are too late to rescue the Doctor and Nasreen as they are captured by the warmongering Restac, and all four of them are held prisoner in the senate.

On the surface, Rory and Tony are stunned to find out that Tony's daughter, Ambrose, has killed their Silurian prisoner whilst attempting to discover an antidote to Tony's sting, and when their monitor screen flares into life and Restac demands that her sister, Alaya, be released, they are unable to comply. Luckily, the execution of Restac's prisoners is delayed by the arrival of Eldane, the elder of the tribe. He agrees to negotiate peace with the humans, sending transports to the surface to collect Rory, Tony and Ambrose. But when they arrive with Alaya's body, chaos engulfs the senate, enhanced by the revelation that Tony and Ambrose have programmed the drill to destroy the oxygen shell around the city.

Restac begins to revive an army of hibernating warriors to prepare for an invasion of the surface, and although the Doctor can stop the drill, he fears that war will break out between the two species. But Eldane has faith in the Doctor and volunteers to perform a toxic fumigation of his city, driving the warriors back into hibernation for another thousand years. Reluctantly, the Doctor agrees, but as the group head back to the TARDIS, Rory is shot by a doomed Restac. As he dies, his body is absorbed by the white light of the crack in the universe, through which the Doctor retrieves a shattered piece of the TARDIS.

As Amy loses all memory of her fiancé's existence, the Doctor's worst fears begin to be confirmed...

Vincent and the Doctor

When the Doctor takes Amy to the Musee D'Orsay to see an exhibition of paintings by Vincent van Gogh, he is startled to find the figure of an alien creature in a picture entitled *The Church at Auvers*, recognising it to be the villain of a Gallifreyan childhood fairy tale.

They travel back to 1890 to investigate and are united with the down-on-his-luck painter. He is regarded as mad by the other citizens of the town. But before the Doctor and Amy can befriend Vincent, a young girl is murdered in the street, and the Doctor urges Vincent to paint the picture that would feature the alien menace as soon as possible, so that they can prevent further bloodshed.

That night, the creature returns and the pair are shocked to realise that it is completely invisible to everybody except van Gogh. The Doctor rigs up a visual recognition device that will help him see the monster, but when they visit the church the next day his plan to stun the beast and return it home falls apart and instead the creature is accidentally killed by the horrified painter.

As a parting gift, the Doctor takes van Gogh to the Musee D'Orsay in the future to show him the legend he will become.

The Big Bang

Two thousand years later, a young Amelia Pond looks up at the pitch blackness of the night sky and dreams of the existence of stars. The next day a strange man in a fez drops a flyer through her door about an exhibition at the National Museum and she asks her aunt Sharon to take her. In the centre of the exhibit is the Pandorica.

In 1AD, Rory cradles a dying Amy in his arms and is surprised to see the Doctor's future self appear in front of him wearing a fez. He instructs Rory to open the Pandorica and release him, putting Amy in his place, before promptly vanishing again. With the Doctor free, he explains that the Pandorica needs to scan the young Amelia's living DNA to restore her to life, which means that Amy has to stay locked in the prison for two thousand years. So for two thousand years, the Auton Rory guards the Pandorica as it travels the world, until he too ends up in the National Museum on the day the Doctor rescues River Song and plans to restore the dead universe.

With Amy safe and sound, the Doctor explains that the inside of the Pandorica holds the only collection of atoms from the original universe in existence. Its restoration field might be barely strong enough to restore Amy, but if he combines it with the exploding TARDIS in the sky above, the power should be enough to re-extrapolate a second Big Bang.

As the Doctor sacrifices himself, the world disintegrates and Amy wakes up on the morning of her wedding to a human Rory with her parents alive and well, and the strangest feeling that she's forgotten something…

As the ceremony is about to begin, Amy Pond remembers the Doctor and the energy she absorbed from the crack in her wall restores the TARDIS in the middle of the church and the Doctor steps out, alive once more.

The Ultimate Honeymoon!

When Amy and Rory finally married, the Doctor prepared to bid them farewell, assuming that the couple might be keen to settle down after the events of the previous night. But he couldn't have been more wrong; before the celebrations were over, Amy and Rory boarded the TARDIS, ready to say goodbye to Earth and continue their travels with the Doctor through the universe as man and wife!

Spoilers

No matter how tempting it might have been, the Doctor has never looked inside River Song's diary. He knows that they are destined to have many more adventures together, and from what River said when she confronted him after Amy and Rory's wedding, it appears that the time is approaching when he will finally find out who she really is. That, she says, is when everything changes…

The Daleks

The Daleks are back, and they're bigger and more dangerous than ever! With the Progenitor in their hands, it can't be long before a new Dalek Army is ready to terrorise the galaxies once more!

The Silence

The Doctor might have solved the mystery of the crack in the universe and the Pandorica, but there are still many unanswered questions. What made the TARDIS explode in Amy's garden on that particular date? And what, exactly, is the Silence that the Doctor has been told will fall?

Right Here, Right Now

The Doctor's busy lifestyle means that it's not often he gets time to dwell on what the future holds, and right now River's secrets, the Silence and the Daleks will all have to wait, because there's an Egyptian goddess loose on the Orient Express… In space!

GOODBYE LEADWORTH, HELLO EVERYTHING!

THE ELEVENTH DOCTOR

Era:	2010+
Number of Companions:	2+
Number of Adventures:	11+
Favoured Accessory:	Bow Tie